BROTHER
with Benefits

MIA CLARK

ISBN: 1511559675
ISBN-13: 978-1511559676

Book design by Cerys du Lys
Cover design by Cerys du Lys
Cover Image © Depositphotos | avgustino

Cherrylily.com

DEDICATION

Thank you to Ethan and Cerys for helping me with this book and everything involved in the process. This is a dream come true and I wouldn't have been able to do it without them. Thank you, thank you!

CONTENTS

ACKNOWLEDGMENTS

Thank you for taking a chance on my book!

I know that the stepbrother theme can be a difficult one to deal with for a lot of people for a variety of reasons, and so I took that into consideration when I was writing this. While this is a story about forbidden love, it's also a story about two people becoming friends, too. Sometimes you need someone to push you in your life, even when you think everything is fine. Sometimes you need someone to be there, even when you don't know how to ask them to stay with you.

This is that kind of story. It is about two people becoming friends, and then becoming lovers. The forbidden aspects add tension, but it's more than that, too. Sometimes opposites attract in the best way possible. I hope you enjoy my books!

STEPBROTHER WITH BENEFITS

1 - *Ashley*

I STRIP DOWN BEFORE opening the door to Ethan's bathroom. I don't know why, it just seems like the right thing to do. And then I open the door, and he's standing there in the shower. He doesn't see me at first, so I just watch him.

He's hard. He's standing there, rinsing off his hair, letting soap and water slide down his body, while his erection bobs and bounces between his legs. Is that how men are?

I don't know. I've never thought to think about it before, but I guess it makes sense. Supposedly they think about sex all the time, right? In which case...

Ethan notices me looking at him, and I avert my eyes, turning away from him. Sort of. I can still see him out of the corner of my eye, watching me, his cock flexes and throbs, no longer bouncing. It's pointing straight at me, like it's latched onto my scent and it plans on moving in for the kill.

Well, that's what I came here for, isn't it?

Gaining some courage despite my reluctance and fear, I step into the bathroom. I've come too far, I'm already here, I'm the one who decided to strip, and now I'm going to go through with this. I close the door behind me just as Ethan opens the sliding shower door and openly admires my body. His eyes move from my toes, to my calves, my thighs, resting for a long while between my legs, then up my stomach, my breasts, and finally, after taking his fill of me, he looks me directly in the eyes.

"Come here," he says with a growl. It's not a request, it's an order.

"Ethan, I..." I stammer and stumble to say something, to make sense of what's going on even though I don't think any of it makes sense. "Can we talk first? Just a little bit."

"What for?" he asks, looking both annoyed and curious.

"I... I want to make sure we both understand the rules of what we're doing."

"Princess, there are no rules here."

"I know," I say. "But I want to make some, if that's alright?"

He doesn't say anything, simply stares at me as water falls all around him, fog floating from the shower stall. I stand in the middle of the bathroom, heat and wetness shimmering across my body. I'm not entirely sure that all this heat is from the shower, though; I know for a fact that the wetness between my legs isn't. But... I need more. I need to talk. Just for a little bit.

"Just a few rules," I say, continuing on. "For example, the first should be that this is only going to last for a week, while Mom and Dad are away."

"Yeah," he says. "Rule number one. Of course."

I nod. "Yes."

"Rule number two," Ethan says. "When I tell you to come here, you come here."

It's still an order, still practically growling at me, commanding me to obey him, but it's more, too. It's fun and flirty, a little playful. I can see why girls fall for him, can see why his devious smirk melts their resistance, because it's doing the same to me.

I go. It's a rule now, and so I have to, don't I? The thought makes me smile. Slow, quiet, I step across the soft bath mat, to the shower. Ethan offers me his hand, wet and strong and desirous, and I take it. He helps me into the shower with him, enveloping me in his world, a world of lust and fog.

He pulls me close and I can feel his erection pressed between us, tight, sliding up along my stomach. His lips kiss at my cheek, towards my ear, and he nibbles softly on my earlobe, then whispers.

"You can change your mind," he says. "Not just now. Whenever. That's rule number three."

"You can, too," I say. "Rule number four."

His hand slides down the curves of my body, towards my hips, my ass. He squeezes hard, pulling me against him, and I can feel him pulse and throb between us. Is he going to take me right here and now? That's what this means, doesn't it? My stepbrother, with benefits?

His hand slips around, caressing past my thigh, heading between my legs. He pulls up, dragging his fingers across my sex, and I shiver and shudder beneath his touch. Yesssss... this is why I came here. This is what I want.

"This is cute," he says. "Trimmed, right?"

I don't understand what he means at first, but then his fingers twirl through my short-cropped pubic hair and I realize it. I nod. "Yes."

"Rule number five," he says. "We're shaving it. Now. I'll do it."

"Um..." I bite my bottom lip, confused.

"Listen, Princess," he says. "I don't mind it. It's nice. You're sexy as fuck, and I will gladly fuck you any which way, but I'm going to shave you bare so that I can show you some things you'll never forget. Got it?"

"Like what?" I ask.

I'm curious, and I wish I knew what he meant, but I really don't. Yes, I'm intelligent, and, yes, I have perfect grades, but this is Ethan's domain, not mine. This is something he can teach me, something I'd never learn in a classroom.

"Sit," he says, slowly guiding me towards the shower wall.

There are steps, or stools I guess you could call them. I have them in my shower in my bathroom off of my bedroom, too. They're for relaxing, or sitting, shaving, that sort of thing. They're built into the wall of the shower, near the rear and the front. He leads me towards one, forcing me down. I go, knees buckling, trembling at the excitement of being trapped in a shower with...

Ethan Colton. My stepbrother. The bad boy every girl wants, the one no one can have; at least not for long...

I know this, but it's fine. We're not in this for the long run. It's just a week. Stepbrother with benefits. It's just...

"Spread your legs," he says, and I do. He reaches for an aerosol can of shaving cream and a fresh razor, then stoops between my legs.

"I'm not sure how I feel about this," I say. "I can do this myself?" It's kind of a question, but I've never done this before, so who knows? Has he done this before? With someone else?

I don't want to think about that right now. I don't want to think about what Ethan has or hasn't done with other girls. I only want to think about what he's going to do with me. To me... what I'll do with him.

"I want to do it," he says, sliding a finger up and down my sex. He pulls it away and sticks it in his mouth, tasting. "Fuck, you're wet, Princess. You excited?"

I nod, accepting it, admitting it. "Yes."

"Good," he says with a grin. "Once you're shaved, I'll take real good care of you."

He sprays foam shaving cream into his hand, then gently brings it between my legs. I gasp at the sudden coolness of it, then shiver at the way he spreads it around. It's nice. This... this is sexual, but I can imagine doing it in a non-sexual way, too. It feels good.

I don't know why I think this. It's stupid and I know it. But I have a sudden urge to ask him if this is included? In our friends with benefits week? What if I want him to shave me down there later? Not for sexual reasons, but just because I... well, he seems to know what he's doing.

Ethan spreads my legs even further while kneeling between them. Slow and steady, he brings the razor to the top of my pubis, then carefully glides it down. The shaving cream smooths away, my trimmed pubic hair going with it, leaving soft, bare skin in its wake. He does this, covering all of the major spots at first, and then he rubs more foam shaving cream in his hands and...

Pulls. Plies. Ethan pulls and plies my sexual curves, my labia, spreading shaving cream every-where. Slow and gentle, dabbing it, covering every inch of hair between my legs. This... this is quite a bit more sexual. I close my eyes and tilt my head back, languishing in the feel. His fingers tease and rub at my clit, making slow circles. I stiffen, opening my mouth wide.

"Ethan..." I breathe, murmuring his name.

"Soon, Princess," he says. "Let me finish this."

He keeps going. He's very good at this. Like an art form almost. That's the only way I can think to describe it. Ethan pulls lightly at my labia, then glides the razor this way and that, over and over, shifting, smoothing, caressing. I've never done this, because I'm always so worried I'll cut myself, but apparently Ethan knows exactly what he's doing, and everything comes out soft and smooth, bare and nice.

"Rule number six," he says. "This is supposed to be fun, Ashley. Understand?"

I nod, trying to agree with him, but lost in thought, too.

"I'm being serious," he says. "Yeah, we're going to fuck. A lot. Hard. But if you don't like something, let me know. We don't have to do anything you don't want to do. If you want to try something, let me know, too. We can give it a shot. Either way, I promise I'll make you feel good. That's what this is all about, got it?"

I nod again, but this time I open my eyes and look down at him. He's staring between my legs, moving the razor, shaving me with expert, focused precision. It's so strange to see Ethan Colton--*the* Ethan Colton--concentrating like this. I've always thought of him as somewhat of a slacker, just someone who screwed around and coasted through life, but for some reason, right now, he looks entirely different to me.

I guess it's not actually that strange, though. I always had a feeling he had some driving passion, and it makes sense that it would involve women.

Not women, some nagging thought at the back of my mind says. You.

That's not true, though. Obviously it's not, and of course it's not. This is just something we're doing for a week. Something that happened because of a stupid mistake. Was it actually that stupid, though? Well, if it was, I'm about to make it again, except this time without the help of alcohol.

I'm excited. I want to know what it feels like. I want to remember all of it, not from the hazy-minded view I had last night, but from the bright, fresh perspective of a new morning to a new day.

"What do you mean by trying something new?" I ask.

"You ever suck cock before, beautiful?" he asks. "You ever deepthroat a guy?"

"What!" I blush and look away from him.

Yes, the irony isn't lost on me. Ethan is shaving my crotch, so him asking me if I've ever given a blowjob should kind of be par for the course, but... it's just the way he says it. So casual and regular, like he has these conversations all the time. I've never heard him talk like this before.

"I'll take that as a no, and a no," he says with a sly grin.

"I have," I say, indignant. No, I haven't. I don't know why I tell him I have.

He stops. He places the razor aside, then lifts up his hand, grabbing my chin. Squeezing slightly, forcing me to look at him, he says, "Rule number seven. Don't lie to me about this shit, Princess. It's not a big deal, alright? I don't care what you've done before. It doesn't matter. It's about what you want to do. Understand?"

I nod slightly, at least as much as I can with my chin in his grip. Ethan steps up, swoops in, and he...

He kisses me. Hard. It's so fast and sudden that I don't realize it at first, and by the time I open my mouth to kiss him back, he stops and goes back to his knees. My mouth hangs open, eyes closed, tongue lolling out, finally prepared to kiss him, but Ethan's already back to finishing with my intimate shave.

I frown, pouting somewhat, wanting to kiss him, but he's busy again already.

"I don't know about the deepthroat thing," I say. "No one's ever let me give them a blowjob before, though. It was just all sex. I mean, I haven't had a lot of sex, but that's all it's been."

"Let me guess," he says. "Missionary? Nothing different?"

I nod, somewhat embarrassed. "I know that's not a lot. I'm sure you've had a ton more experience."

I know he's had a ton more experience. There's really no question there.

Ethan shrugs and flashes me a brilliant smile. I melt. It's so soft and nice, but sexy and deliberate, too.

"Doesn't matter. This isn't about that. This is just two people enjoying each other," he says. "Yeah, we'll be naked, but whatever. Fun is fun, right?"

"I'm not so sure about that," I say, smiling a little. "Haven't you ever wanted more, Ethan?"

"More?" he asks, furrowing his brow.

"You know, um... like a girlfriend? Something more? Not just sex?"

"Not really," he says. "Not sure why you're asking me this."

Belatedly I realize what it sounds like. Like I want more with him? Which is obviously impossible. He's still my stepbrother, regardless of what we've decided.

We? Is this something we decided together? Yes, sort of.

"I don't know," I say. "I didn't mean anything by it."

Ethan grunts. That's that, apparently.

He finishes up. I'm completely shaven now, absolutely bare. It feels kind of nice. For good measure, he slaps at my bare skin, smacking my pussy. I jump from the sudden jolt of sensation, but he just laughs. "Sensitive, huh?"

"It's... it's different."

"You'll like it," he says. "Let me do me quick, then we'll see what happens."

I get the distinct feeling he isn't going to leave this up to fate, though. This isn't a wait and see type of situation.

"You... um... you're shaving, too?" I ask.

"Yeah," he says with a shrug. He sprays shaving foam in his hands, then slathers it around his cock, near the base of his shaft, and his balls.

Surprisingly, or not, he's still absurdly hard. I can see him now, up close and personal, and... he's large. I've never really gotten a good look at a penis before now, but Ethan definitely has something to be proud of. I inadvertently find myself staring.

He laughs. "Like what you see, Princess?"

I nod. No lying, right? Rule number seven. "I don't think I can ever deepthroat that," I say.

"You'd be surprised what you can do if you really want to," he says with a grin. "There's some tricks to it. I'll teach you if you want."

"What?" Tricks? Really? I would have thought my throat and my mouth was only so big...

"To get past your gag reflex," he says. "Some girls are more sensitive to it than others, but there's a trick."

He holds up his left hand, showing me, then pulls his thumb towards his palm, wraps his fingers around it, and squeezes. I follow along, or I think I do, but he shakes his head.

"Left hand, Ashley. If you squeeze your left thumb, it helps stop your gag reflex. You can take a lot more in that way. You still need to practice, but that's the best way to start."

"Really?" I ask, squeezing my left thumb.

"Really," he says. "You want to find out first hand?"

His smirk is infectious, and the way his cock bounces, it's like just thinking about me sucking his cock has him excited. I suppose that might be the truth, too.

"Do *you* want to?" I ask, grinning.

"You're asking me if I want my cock deep in your throat? Yeah, if that's what you're asking, I damn well fucking would love it. I'll practice that shit with you until you're a pro."

I laugh. "You make it sound so dirty."

"It's pretty fucking dirty," he says, and he laughs, too.

"Why are you shaving yourself?" I ask, suddenly curious.

"It's nice," he says. "When we're both shaved, it's nice. Real smooth. Slippery, especially when you're really wet, which I hope to fuck you'll be. If not, it's cool. We can use lube or something. Might have to after awhile."

"Why?"

"Ashley, I don't know if you get this yet, but a week is a long fucking time, and you can have a whole lot of sex in that amount of time. I'm being completely honest when I say I plan to take full advantage of that. I'm going to be hard all fucking week for you, Princess."

My God... he's just so... I don't even know. So enchanting. In the dirtiest, naughtiest of ways. This isn't supposed to be that exciting. At least I didn't think it was, but, no, it is. It's more exciting than I thought.

I'm glad I came up here. I'm glad I decided to accept his offer. I realize how strange this sounds. This is Ethan, he's... he's my stepbrother. It's weird. Maybe it's gross. Disgusting. I would agree if someone said that, too.

But, it's us. It's our secret. Just for a week. And Ethan is fun. It's like he's mine for a week. I get to experience everything that all of those other girl's have experienced, but different, too. None of them got to live with him, now did they? I doubt any of them ever had the chance to eat breakfast with him like I did. And it won't even just be today.

I bet he never offered to have a night in with them while watching a movie and eating pizza and getting drunk. It was a mistake, what happened after that, sort of, but...

Maybe it wasn't? I'm not sure anymore.

"Let's practice," he says. "Come here, Princess."

Rule number two: when Ethan says come here, I go.

He's standing there. Finished. His cock is smooth and shiny, soft and bare. It looks... a little strange at first, but somewhat mesmerizing, too. Slick and shimmering, like some shining treasure of lust. I move to stand and go to him, but he shakes his head.

"On your knees, Princess. I want to see Little Miss Perfect take my cock in her mouth."

It's weird, because I've always heard him say these things in a mean way. I always thought he was rude and arrogant, but the way he says it now, it sounds... almost fun. Playful? Still a little arrogant, but in a sexy sort of way. Well, two can play at that game.

I toss my hair back over my shoulder and roll my eyes at him, nonchalant. He stares down at me, smirking.

"Take your time, beautiful. There's no rush. Just get used to--"

Before he can finish, I'm on him. Left thumb, squeeze, yes, I do that. I use my other hand to grab the base of his cock, and then I open my mouth wide, kiss his crown, and push my way down. I can feel him, feel him on my tongue and in my mouth. He's wet from having rinsed off his cock after shaving, which probably helps a lot, but I can't think about that right now.

I go. I just keep going. I feel him pressing against the back of my throat as far as I can go, as far as I would usually go before gagging; though I've never done this with a cock, but I know from um... just having brushed my teeth? It's kind of like the same thing, right?

No, not really. His finger trick really does work, too. I keep going, or I try to.

"Holy fucking shit," Ethan says. "That's a beautiful fucking sight, Princess."

I swirl my tongue around the underside of his shaft, then I pull back. "Was that good?" I ask.

"Yeah," he says. "Fuck. You want to try something?"

"What?"

"Here's how this works, alright? If it's too much, slap the back of my thigh. Any thigh, any amount of slapping. As hard as you want. Really get my attention with it."

"What?"

"You're going to do that again, and once you're as far as you can go, I'm going to help you out a little. Understand?" He smiles, soft, and he actually looks really nice right now; not just sexy and handsome, but like he's not an asshole.

I'm not sure if it's because I'm about to put his cock back in my mouth or what, but apparently Ethan can be nice when he wants to be.

"I'll try it," I say. I like this. It's fun and interesting in its own way. I like the feel of him in my mouth, too. It's a new experience, and it's definitely one I'd like to experience again in the future.

"When you get as far as you can, I'm going to keep pulling you more," he says. "I'll go slow, but let's see how much of my cock you can take. If it hurts or if you can't breathe, you just slap my thigh, alright? Don't forget."

I nod, listening, ready. I can do this. I wonder how it will feel?

I go. I begin. I start out much like I did before, but without my hand on the base of his cock this time. Instead, I grab the backs of his thighs, almost like I'm pulling myself forward. When the head of his cock gets close to my gag reflex, I do Ethan's thumb trick, and go even further. There. That's it. I...

He wraps his fingers in my hair, grabbing fistfuls. His fingertips press against the back of my head, squeezing slightly, and then, ever so slowly, he begins to pull me further onto him. I can... oh God, I can feel it! I can feel him in me, in my throat. I tilt my head slightly, just so. Yes, that's how um... wow.

I swallow, because it feels like I have to swallow something, and Ethan's cock twitches and vibrates in my mouth.

"Yeah, that's it," he says. "Fuck, that feels so goddamn good. You want to keep going? Tap the back of my leg lightly if you do. Let me know, Princess."

Do I? Yesss... I tap his leg lightly, just a little, then I grab again.

He pulls me, pulls me more. How much of him can I take? My eyes start to water and a slip of drool slides down my lips, my chin, mixing with the water from the shower. We're in the back of the shower stall, with Ethan blocking the brunt of the water, but I can still feel it splashing on my hands and pooling slightly near my knees and feet.

"Shit," he says. "Holy fucking shit. You've almost got it. Just a little more and you'll have my entire cock in your mouth. Remember, Princess, just slap me hard if you want to stop."

No, I don't want to. I want to do this. It's weird, but I like the way he says this. Like I'm good, like he's praising me. I guess I'm still a good girl in some ways, even if what we're doing is incredibly wrong and naughty. I want this. I want to be Ethan's good girl.

In some ways I need it because we only have a week.

I don't realize it when I'm lightheaded, but Ethan must. He pulls me back, sliding me away. I cough and choke at first, but he lifts me up and off the shower floor. He pulls me close to him, embracing me, cradling me in his arms. Kissing me. Oh my God, he's kissing me again.

I catch my breath, and even though I know my eyes are red and I must look strange, it doesn't matter to him. He kisses me, pulling me close to him. I give in to him, too. My hands cup his cheeks and I kiss him back. I feel his erection between us, bouncing and slapping at my stomach. Reaching down, I wrap my fingers around his shaft and stroke slightly.

"I don't even know what you do to me," he says, almost whispering. "You're like a fucking drug, Ashley. I can't get enough of you."

I smile and stroke him a little more, but he breaks away from our kiss.

"Fuck this," he says. "We're done. Shower's over."

Without a second's hesitation, he turns off the shower. The water slows to a stop, leaving us naked and wet. Towels? Ethan grabs one, flings it over his shoulder, then he grabs me.

I shriek and laugh as he lifts me up, handling my ass, pulling me to him. I wrap my legs around his waist, painfully aware of how easy it would be for him to just slide me a little bit lower, how quickly he could pull me onto his throbbing cock. Ethan carries me towards the sliding shower door, pulls it open, then lifts me up even higher and brings me to the door to his bedroom.

I open it for him, peeking over my shoulder to grab the doorhandle.

His bed. He's bringing me to his bed. Lightly, he places me back on the floor at the side of his bed, then he flips the towel he brought, making a space for us both. I think that's what he's doing, at least. I'm really not sure until...

He grabs me again. Lifts me up. This time he does it. He slides me down, fitting me perfectly onto his cock. He fills me halfway, then he falls onto the bed with me beneath him. My back crashes against his mattress, the box spring squeaking beneath us, and then Ethan slams the rest of the way inside of me, filling me completely.

Like that. Oh, yes, just like that. He pulls out and thrusts back in. Hard. Fast. I can feel it, feel everything. Oh God, he's right. This is amazing. So sensitive and soft and slick, my bare body sliding against his.

He sucks on my neck, teeth biting lightly at my flesh, grunting hard as he slams his cock deep inside of me.

There's... wait... I need to remember this. I remember just in time, and while I don't even want to do this, I do it. I slap and push at him, trying to get him to stop, to pay attention, to...

"Ethan," I say. "Ethan, stop for a second. You need to stop. We need to use a condom. I saw them. You have them in the drawer in your bedside table."

"Rule number fucking eight," he says, growling into my ear. "No condoms, Ashley. Not this week. You're on birth control, and we both know it, so I want to take full advantage of that. This pussy is mine."

"Ethan! I'm being serious! You..."

I feel bad thinking this. Because I love what's going on. I love his cock inside me. I even loved how it felt last night when he filled me, and I really do want to know how it feels again when we're both more level headed, but...

He has a lot more experience than me, and I know I've always used condoms, and...

He stops, sort of. He's still inside me, but he's not thrusting. He kisses me lightly on the lips, then the tip of my nose.

"I know what you think of me," he says. "I don't blame you. Everyone probably thinks it. My dad does, too. He makes me get tested every month, no matter what. I have to or he'll cut off my trust fund money. It's part of our agreement. I'm clean, Ashley. I swear. I wouldn't do that to you. I know this might come as a shock, but I haven't had sex since I last got tested months ago, either. Too busy focusing on football and keeping up my grades."

"Really?" I ask. "You've been studying?"

I smile, and he laughs, which makes me laugh, too.

"Yeah, crazy, huh?"

"Ethan Colton, studying..." I say, like this is some insane, awe-inspiring fact. It is a little insane, though maybe not awe-inspiring. "Are you doing well at college?"

"Yeah," he says. "Probably not as good as you. Mostly high Cs, but I got a B+ in World Mythology."

"World Mythology? You're taking that as a class? I don't know if I believe it."

"I know all there is to know about fertility goddesses," he says. "Trust me."

I laugh. He smiles down at me. I close my eyes for a second, and when I open them he gives me a light kiss.

"Everyone knows you're a bad boy, Ethan," I say. "Can I really trust you?"

"I want you to trust me," he says. "No lying, remember? That's one of the rules."

"Rule number seven," I say, nodding.

"Shit, you even remembered the number," he says with a smirk.

"Mhm," I hum. "And rule number eight... no condoms..."

That's it. That's all he needs. I trust him. I didn't know about his father, or the testing, or the trust fund money. It's interesting and gives me a different perspective, a different view into the life of Ethan Colton.

My stepbrother. Who is currently slamming his cock hard into me, deep inside of me, my greedy and rebellious body giving in to his lusty demands. I'm the good girl, right? I want to be good for him.

He's.... he's mine--I mean, he's my stepbrother, that is. He's Ethan. We're... friends? With benefits. It's confusing. Complicated. I don't fully understand it, myself, but I like this. I like what's going on. I want it to happen.

No one's ever made me feel like this before, and I love it so much. I love...

I shake my head of that thought as quickly as it started. No, it's not like that. Or, not the same. This is entirely different. I'm just being stupid now, but I don't have time for stupid.

Ethan pulls back, sitting up. He grabs my hips in both of his hands and holds me tight, then thrusts as hard and as fast as he can into me. Our bodies slap together, loud. If anyone else was in the house, I'm sure they could hear us, except they aren't; it's just us. I feel his balls clapping against my ass. It's a weird sensation at first, but I like it.

He presses the palm of one of his hands against my stomach, then teases his thumb down, stroking lightly near my clit. A little more, closer, until I can feel it so much that I start to squirm and writhe on the bed.

"Yeah, fuck," he says. "Just like that. Cum on my cock, Princess. I want to feel it."

What can I say? I'm a good girl. Rule number two: when Ethan tells me to cum, I cum. That's how this works, right?

I've never felt like this before. Never felt so... so alive, so aroused, so full, so... *so many things.*

It doesn't take long. No one's ever cared about my pleasure during sex. Not that I've had a lot of partners to begin with, but still. It's oddly fascinating how much more pleasurable this is with a little extra care. Just a thumb? Light, even circles, pressing just the right buttons on my body, and...

My climax overtakes me and I squeeze and clench, my entire body, inside and out. Ethan's cock forces its way inside of me even while my body seems desperate to squeeze him out. He shoves in hard, and I can feel him twitching, feel myself clenching, feel him...

While my orgasm drives a million streaks of pleasure through my sinfully slick body, Ethan cums inside of me. I can feel it, feel his warmth and his seed. He's deep, *very* deep. It feels nice. *Very* nice.

This is how it's supposed to feel, I think. This is what I've been missing. This is what...

Ethan crashes down onto me, squishing me. I giggle, because he makes a show of being exhausted. Why do I get the feeling that Ethan Colton is anything but exhausted? He pants and breathes hard into my neck, then kisses me lightly.

"Holy fuck," he says. "You're amazing."

"Am I?" I ask, smiling and tilting my head so I can kiss him. "You're amazing, too. That was amazing."

He squeezes me tight in his arms, hugging me. I'm not sure if we're going to stay like that or get up, but I like this. It's... it's close. Like cuddling, but with his cock still inside of me after we've just had sex. I can still feel him twitch and throb. I do a few practice squeezes. Like um... like Kegels? I squeeze his cock with my inner walls, my muscles, and I feel him twitch and throb in response.

"Cut that shit out," he says. "We'll never get out of bed if you keep it up."

I do it again, smiling wide at him.

"Oh, we've got a fucking sex freak here, do we? You deepthroat my cock on the first try and then fuck like a goddamn Sex Queen and now you think you can try and get a rise out of me? Nah, I don't think so, Ashley."

He pulls out of me and stands up suddenly. I try to grab him, to pull him back, but he refuses. His cock is... wow... he's still quite erect. A little soft, but much harder than I would have expected. Granted, my experience is basically um... a few men who were done in a minute or so, who were soft and with their pants back on in half that time, so...

Ethan doesn't bother with pants. He casually walks into the bathroom, buck naked, cock swinging side to side, and grabs a washcloth from the sink countertop. He turns on the hot water, soaks the cloth, then comes back to me. Gentle and sweet, oddly caring, he slides the cloth from the bottom of my stomach, down my sex, towards my ass, cleaning me.

I wriggle beneath him, caught up in the sensation. Yes, it's cleaning, but... he's rubbing a warm, wet cloth across my clit and my labia and... it feels nice. I like it.

"What are you doing?" I ask.

"Mine," he says. "This is my pussy for the week, and I'm doing proper maintenance on it."

"I'm not a car, Ethan," I say, laughing.

"Nah, I know," he says. "I'm still gonna ride the fuck out of you, though, Princess."

God! He's so... so horrible, and yet so amazing, too. The things he says are so wrong, but for some reason I love them. I like being the center of his attention. I really do. I like it a lot.

I think I could get used to this, and I'd love to try, but then the doorbell rings. A second later someone pushes the buzzer.

Ethan looks at me funny. "You expecting someone?"

I give him a look that's much the same. "Um...?"

He shrugs. The buzzer is part of the intercom system, and we each have one in all of our rooms. We can turn it on or off to talk to someone from another room or someone at the front gates. Ethan leaves me naked and wet, laying on his bed, and goes to the intercom near his door, then presses the call button.

"Hey," he says. "Who is it?"

"Um... is Ashley home?" someone asks. "It's me. Julia. She texted me last night and said to come over so we could hang out."

Oh, shit. I almost forgot. Panic flashes through my eyes and I sit up straight, suddenly fully realizing that um...

I'm naked in my brother's bed. We just had sex. Stepbrother, I remind myself.

Yes, well, that's not all that much better and I certainly can't tell Julia about this...

"She's getting dressed or some shit," Ethan says into the intercom. "I'll go tell her you're here. I'll be right down to let you in."

"Um... thanks?" Julia says, nervous, practically squeaking.

Yes, she knows Ethan, too. We all went to school together. She knows exactly how he is, and how frightening he can be. He's definitely made a reputation for himself.

Ethan turns to me and grins. "We're done for now, Princess. Apparently you've got a visitor."

Done? Because if Julia hadn't shown up we... wouldn't have been done? A quick glance towards Ethan's crotch seems to agree with this.

He's hard. Harder than hard. He definitely does not look like he's just had sex. With me. He came inside me. Then cleaned me. His pussy, he said. I'm his.

For a week. My stepbrother with benefits.

Oh God, what did I agree to? This is a dangerous game to play...

2 - Ethan

WHILE ASHLEY GOES TO CLEAN UP and put some clothes on, apparently it's my job to play host to her friend, Julia. Well, fuck.

I kind of wish she hadn't done that. Because, going to be honest here, I'm nowhere near done with Ashley yet. Not even close. I've got a week to get this shit out of my system, and I plan to take full advantage of that.

Is that what this is then? Getting it out of my system?

Nah.

Alright, maybe a little bit. Who the fuck knows?

It's supposed to be for her, too, to show Ashley what's up, to give her some experience and teach her what a guy who's actually into her can be like. Which I am. Fuck, I'm into her alright. Holy shit this girl is my stepsister. I don't know what I'm thinking right now. This is messed up. Yeah, alright, but who cares?

Not me. Not exactly. Her pussy is fine as hell and I plan to take full advantage of my week with her. It's just...

This whole thing is more complicated than I first thought. To be fair, I didn't even think about it much, though. Friends with benefits? Yeah, that works great when you can stop, when once it's all done you can just go your separate ways and never bother with the person again.

Ashley lives in the same house as me. We're stuck here together for the rest of the summer. Once her mom and my dad come back from vacation, how's that going to work? Future planning isn't exactly my strong suit if you couldn't tell.

I'll just leave. Go on vacation like Ashley thought I would. She can have the house to herself for the rest of the summer, or as much to herself as she can with our parents hanging around, too. Not that they really count for this, since I'm the one fucking her and that's the reason it's going to be awkward.

Maybe. Who knows? I'll play it by ear, see how it goes. Maybe it'll be fine. Not that I give a shit, because I don't. Ashley's the one I'm worried about.

Worried? What the fuck bullshit is this? I don't even know.

Anyways, I have stuff to do. Get the fuck out of my head.

I head downstairs and go to the front door, then walk towards the front gate. Going to invite the girl in all personal-like, be a good host, whatever. Yeah, I could just hit a buzzer and open the gate for her, but I need some time to think and a short walk sounds good.

Except I forgot my shirt. Not really. I didn't wear a shirt on purpose, and it doesn't bother me, but when Julia sees me walking to the gate to let her in, her jaw drops. The pretty bitch just stands there, staring at me, practically salivating over my ripped abs. Yeah, that's right. I work out. Sexy as fuck, and don't you forget it.

I'm not trying to be. I didn't plan on this. It's not like I want to hook up with my sister's friend or anything. Not that I have anything against it, either, but this isn't supposed to be like that.

Well, fuck, she's still staring at me.

I open the gate and let her in, and she stammers out some words of thanks.

"Umm... thanks... hey, Ethan," Julia says.

"Hey, what's up?" I say. You know, common greeting, right?

This chick takes it super seriously. I didn't mean to start a full on conversation here, but whatever.

"Oh, just going to hang out with Ashley. She texted me last night. I would have come over, but she said you two were having a movie night together? That's so nice of you! I wish I had a brother like you that I could hang out with."

By that, I'm pretty sure she means she wishes she had man candy to stare at, because going by the way she can't keep her eyes off my abs, she's not at all interested in just hanging out with someone like me. Yeah, she wants the D. Oh well, what can you do?

"Yeah," I say. "She's inside. Let's go."

Julia starts following me like some lovesick puppy dog, which is probably pretty close to the truth. I don't know why this shit happens to me. I mean, no, I know why it happens, and I should have put a shirt on or something, but it probably would have happened either way. Once we step inside it gets even worse.

Holy fuck, girl, my eyes are up here. Yeah, the air conditioner is on, and, yeah, my man nips are hard. It's natural. Biology or whatever. I'm just not that into you. I'm sure I could have sex with this girl if I wanted to. It wouldn't be hard. She's pretty cute, decent body, probably into it. I like her voice, too. That's important, alright? When a girl screams your name while you're thrusting into her, pounding the fuck out of her, naked and covered in sweat, you want it to sound nice.

"Ethan! Ethan! Yes! More! Ethan! Yes!"

Yeah, I bet Julia would be good at that. I can believe it.

"You look different," she says, putting a hand on my bicep. "You play football, right? I know you did in high school but do you still play in college?"

"Yeah," I say. "Quarterback. We went 11-1 this year. Good season."

"So you won eleven games?" she asks.

Uh, yeah, that's exactly what that means...

I think I'm supposed to be polite right now, though. This is Ashley's friend, so it makes sense. Why the fuck does she keep touching my bicep? Chicks always do this. I don't get it. Do I walk up to them and just start copping a feel, groping their breasts? Nah, I don't think so. I wouldn't mind, though. Maybe I'll try it sometime.

And then she moves to the abs. It's like a fucking script, preplanned. I could have told you all of this would happen. Yeah, where's my shirt? I don't fucking know. Ashley's the smart girl. Why the fuck didn't she tell me to put my shirt on? I'm blaming this on her.

"So... do you have a girlfriend?" Julia asks. "I've just been um... curious. Not for any reason. I'm single, myself. Haven't met any nice guys yet, so..."

I have no clue what that means. I'm definitely not a nice guy. I mean, obviously she wants my cock, but that still doesn't make me a nice guy. Well, whatever. Let's just go with it.

Because, yeah, you know what? I just realized this, but it's important. Friends with benefits. With Ashley. For a week. And then what? I need a way to break it off. I need Ashley to know what a prick I am, to want nothing to do with me. It's going to be hard. For her. Not me. I've done this a million times before. No big deal.

I think Julia is the answer, though. When I'm done with Ashley, I'll *coincidentally* start hanging out with Julia, get them both to hate me, then they can hang out together and hate me at the same time. Girl talk. Movie nights. The whole nine yards.

Wait. Wow. Fuck. What if Ashley has a movie night with Julia to get over me, and they both get drunk and... nah. That doesn't happen, does it? Accidental lesbians? Bisexual? Huh...

I'm too lost in my fucked up ideas to realize that Julia's fingers are creeping past the waistband of my pants and we're standing in the middle of the hallway, right by the stairs. My cock is still twitching, ready for some action after leaving Ashley, and I think it's giving this thirsty chick some ideas, too. No clue. It's definitely not just my shirtless abs she's staring at anymore.

3 - Ashley

A FTER ETHAN GOES TO LET JULIA IN, I shower again quick. Nothing too intensive, but I'm sweaty and slick from our sudden steamy fun and I think Julia and I are going out, so I want to smell and look nice. That's the plan, at least, but once I'm in the shower I can't stop thinking about what happened.

It wasn't an accident this time. I knew exactly what I was doing, and...

I'm so smooth! This is strange. I like to keep myself trimmed down there, just because, but after Ethan shaved all of my pubic hair off I'm surprisingly soft and smooth. I keep touching myself, amazed at how nice it feels, but um... it starts to feel nice in more ways than one. I remember how Ethan touched me, how he made me feel, and my fingers kind of end up having a mind of their own. It's startling, but nice, too. It seems natural. I...

I stop. I need to get out of this shower! I need to get dressed! Also, I want to save that. For Ethan. My God, how awful does that sound? I want to save my orgasms for my brother. Weird. Gross.

He's my stepbrother. I don't know why I need to keep reminding myself of that, but I do. It makes this better. Sort of. More understandable. Reasonable and alright, you know? Because we aren't actually related or anything. Just by marriage. It's not like this is actually wrong, it's just a social construct we've built up in our heads. It's something society tells us is unacceptable even though there's technically no reason for it to be.

Maybe if we'd grown up together for... longer... then it would be a lot weirder.

I don't know if that works, either, though. I've known Ethan since second grade, and we weren't stepbrother and sister then, but I still knew him. I *have* grown up with him in a way. Not in the same way, but I know more about him than I care to admit. I know about how he got suspended from school for giving a teacher a box of spiders as a gift. That was kind of funny, actually. Not at the time, and the teacher screamed. Ethan wrapped it up and everything, put a bow on top, and made it seem like an actual present.

They weren't dangerous spiders. Opiliones, sometimes referred to as harvestmen or daddy longlegs. When I was younger, after my dad died, when my mom and I used to sit outside on the porch in the evening at my grandparents house when we were staying there, trying to get back on our feet, they used to come out and skitter around us. I remember being scared at first, but my mom showed me they weren't scary. After that, I used to hold my hand out and sometimes they'd crawl onto my fingers and just stand there, staring at me.

Girls are supposed to be scared of spiders. That's what everyone says. I don't like other spiders, but I like daddy longlegs. I like the way their little legs stretch out, how they seem curious and interested in the world around them. Maybe I'm projecting. I don't know.

After Ethan gave our teacher a box of spiders, she screamed and threw it into the air. The spiders skittered out, surprised. I felt bad for them, and worried, too. A classroom wasn't any place for spiders, especially because they might get hurt. Obviously they weren't going to hurt anyone; it's impossible. I remember running over to help them, to put them back in the box to keep them safe so I could bring them outside...

Another boy in our class stood up to play the hero, or so it seemed. While I stooped to try and gather the spiders back in the box to keep them safe, he lifted up his leg and prepared to stomp on them.

Ethan punched him. Hard. I didn't see it happen, but I heard the other boy's jaw crack and heard the sound of him falling to the ground, crashing against the metal legs of a school desk.

I'm not sure if Ethan got suspended for the spiders or the punch, to be honest. Or maybe a combination of the two. He was almost permanently expelled, but his father donated a sizable sum of money to the school as reparations and they transferred him to another class, too. That was the last day of that school year that I had class with Ethan Colton. I still saw him during recess and lunch, though.

I used to like him, then. I used to think he punched the boy to protect the spiders. And to save me. Not that the other boy meant to hurt me, but my fingers were in the way, or *maybe* they were. I didn't see it all. I...

Wow. How foolish. Why am I thinking about this now? He didn't do any of that for me. Ethan was just a troublemaker. A bad boy. That's how he's always been.

I used to imagine he was looking at me at lunch or during recess, though. Sometimes. Except when I went to look, he never was. He was always turned away. Fast, maybe, like he didn't want me to see him staring. That's what I thought. I don't think that anymore.

I don't *think* I think that, at least.

I dress in a cute patterned skirt and a nice tanktop, trying to forget about the past, to just live in the moment. It doesn't matter if Ethan Colton secretly looked at me years ago during recess, or if he protected me from a boy when I was trying to save the spiders. He's looking at me now. He sees me now, sees me here. Maybe it's not the same as what I used to think... (what I used to want?)

It doesn't matter. It's a week, it's us for a week, and it's enough. It has to be.

With benefits, yes, but I hope Ethan will still be my friend after. Is that too much to ask? Maybe. Maybe he'll think it's a lot. Maybe he won't want that. I don't know if it's possible.

Once I finish putting on my shoes and fix my hair quick in the mirror, I step outside my room and walk down the hall to the stairs. I tried to blow dry my hair as much as I could, but it's still a little wet, and it sticks and clings to the back of my neck and my shirt. My neck prickles and shivers at the feel of it, but...

Oh my God. What's going on? My entire body shivers at what I see when I step down the last stair and turn into the hallway.

Ethan is standing there, near the front door, between the kitchen and the den, right in the middle of the hall, and Julia is there, too. She's clinging to him, close; too close. Her hands are on his abs, his waist, fingers peeking beneath the waistband of his pants. Obviously Ethan is shirtless. I hadn't thought about it when he left to let Julia in, because I kind of just liked staring at him shirtless, but now that I think about it, um...

I clear my throat and glare at the two of them. "Um, excuse me!"

Ethan looks up, brow furrowed, staring at me. "Hey, Ashley," he says.

Julia is a little more circumspect. She pulls her hands out of Ethan's pants and backs away. "Oh, um... hey Ashley. I was just talking to Ethan about college and football and..."

"Sorry, Julia," I say, marching towards the two of them. "I need to borrow my brother for a second. I'll be right back and then we can hang out."

I don't blame Julia. This is obviously Ethan's fault. He's always like this. This is how he's been since forever. Has he slept with her before? I don't think so, but I'm not sure. I like to think that Julia would have told me at some point, but maybe it just never came up. Maybe they're...

Ugh! I can't believe him! With her, right after he... with me? And...

I grab Ethan's arm and drag him down the hall, bringing him into one of the downstairs guest bedrooms. This is a horrible choice of room, but it was the first open one I saw through my raging anger, and it has a door that I can close and lock behind us. Which I do. Loudly. Then I push Ethan. Again. He's stronger than me. This isn't doing anything to him. He doesn't even care. Why is he doing this? Why is he smirking and laughing at me.

"Hey, I think you have the wrong idea," he says.

"Wrong idea?" I ask. "You were flirting with my friend! Right after... after we..."

"Shh, Princess," he says, smirking even more now. "Don't want her hearing, do you?"

"Have you slept with her?" I ask. "Is that it?"

"Nah," he says. Just casual, easy as that. Nah.

"Were you going to? Were you planning on it, Ethan? Because..."

Because why? We're not in a relationship. We're not boyfriend and girlfriend. He has no reason not to sleep with her if he wants to, which, if I know Ethan Colton, means he probably will. He's an asshole like that and I hate him, and...

"Listen, Ashley, I don't know what you think friends with benefits means, but in my world it means you can't get upset about something like that. If you can't handle it, maybe we should just back off and stop this right now."

Maybe we should. I can't exactly disagree with him. It makes sense. It makes sense for us to never have even tried to do this in the first place, too, though. It's just...

Then I remember. I think of something. I don't know if this will work, but it doesn't hurt to try. Right?

"Ethan, we need another rule," I say. "Rule number ten. You can't sleep with any other girls while we're... we're doing what we're doing."

"While we're fucking the shit out of each other and having a good time," he says, smirking.

"I'm being serious!" I say, but the way he smiles, the way he says it so casually, it makes me smile, too. Is that what we did? Fuck the shit out of each other? It sounds crass and rude, but also incredibly accurate.

"Usually I'd tell you to fuck off," he says. "Usually."

"Because you're an asshole," I say, nodding. "Not just usually, but always."

"Yeah," he says, grinning. "I'll give you a break, though. Since we're just in this for a week, I'll follow your rule. Number ten, right? I'll even remember the number, just for you, Princess."

"Shut up," I say.

"Make me," he says.

I do. I make him. I push him, again, and he falls back against the bed. I follow, climbing on top of him, straddling him. My skirt bunches up around the tops my thighs, and Ethan pulls it up even more, lifting it past my waist. While I straddle and sit in his lap as he sits on the guest bed, he cups my ass and pulls me close.

I shut him up. I make him shut up. I press my lips against his and kiss him hard. He kisses me back with more passion and desire than I ever thought possible. I don't know if this is an Ethan Colton thing, or if it's a regular sexual thing, but no one's ever kissed me like this. I've never kissed anyone else like this, either.

His hands slip between my panties and he teases at the smooth, soft folds of my sex with his fingertips, sliding them back and forth. I'm aroused, I realize. I know I am, but I realize it even more as Ethan coats his fingers with my arousal, caressing my wetness back and forth between my thighs. I don't care. I don't care that Julia is in the hallway, that she's expecting me to come out to spend time with her, that she was...

I do what she was doing. Sort of. I trace my fingers down my stepbrother's abs and slip my fingers in his pants. He grins, and slips his fingers in...

In me. One, then another. Pushing, pulling me more into his lap. I open my mouth to gasp, but he stops me by biting my bottom lip.

"Shhh, Princess," he whispers. "Can't be too loud. Don't want your friend to know what's going on, do we?"

"Ethan, I..." I kiss him again, but then I stop, breathing heavy into his ear. "Please don't flirt with another girl this week? Please? I know I shouldn't ask you that. I know it's not within... within..."

Me. His fingers are in me. They're all I can think about right now. I just... I only want them in me. I don't want to think about them being in someone else. I just don't. I know that's irrational and wrong, but I want this to be us, to be enjoyable to the both of us, and I want him to flirt with me. I want him to touch me. I want him to...

I want him to fuck me. To make love to me. To take me, hard. To be soft. Gentle. Careful. To love and hold and handle roughly and...

"You got it, baby girl," he says. "Just for you. I promise."

"It's only for a week," I say, gasping out the words.

"That's the only reason I'm agreeing to it," he says, smirking.

And then, as quick as that, he pulls his fingers out of me, then smacks my ass. The noise echoes through the room. It's loud! I wouldn't be surprised if...

Yup, she heard it.

"Is everything alright in there?" Julia says. "I heard a noise, and--"

She tries to open the door, but it's locked. The doorknob rattles ineffectively, and I know she can't get in, but I still scramble up and off Ethan's lap. Or, I try to. He squeezes me tight, pulls me back close, and sinks his teeth into my neck, nibbling.

"Fuck, I wish you hadn't told her to come over here today," he says. "Why'd you have to do that, Princess?"

"I didn't know," I say, groaning and grinding against him, my crotch finding a delightful spot to press against his hip. "I wouldn't have if..."

"Damn fucking right you wouldn't have," he growls. "You go out and have fun now, but don't forget to think of what's going to happen to you when you get back home."

"What's going to happen?" I ask, both coy and curious. I have a good idea, but...

He flips me off of him and pushes me against the bed, pinning me there with his knee between my legs, keeping them open.

"Hey, um... guys? Is everything alright?" Julia asks.

"Fine," Ethan says, growling at the door. "Go get a glass of fucking milk in the kitchen or something. We're having a serious conversation here."

"Um... sure... sorry..."

I almost laugh, but Ethan stops me by pressing a finger to my lips. And that's not my mouth I'm talking about. He presses a finger past my panties, then to my pussy, then inside me, and...

Curls it. Um... wow, what was that? I just... I felt...

Holy fuck! He does it again, hooking... me? I don't even know what this is. There's something oddly magical going on inside my body and I can't even begin to explain how amazing this is. Intense sensation floods my entire being, my whole state of existence.

"You like that, Princess?" he asks.

I somehow manage to mumble and nod that, yes, I do like that. Quite a lot. A very lot. Yes, much liking, um...

"You ever have anyone eat you out before?" he asks.

I shake my head. "No, um... no one has... I'm curious, but um... it's weird to ask, isn't it?"

"Ask me," he says. "Fucking ask me to do it, Ashley."

Oh God. Is he serious? I blink open my eyes--I didn't even realize I'd closed them--and look at him, and... yes... Ethan looks dreadfully serious. Horrifyingly serious. The most serious I've ever seen him look, actually. It's very intense.

"Will you..." I start to ask. I'm not sure how I'm going to phrase this, but it doesn't matter, because he takes over from there.

"Yeah," he says. "I can't fucking wait. Your pussy is mine, Princess. Don't you forget it. I'm going to devour the fuck out of it later. Think about that while you're off with your friend. You two better fucking leave the house and not tell me where you're going or else I don't know if I can stop myself from going after you, grabbing you, throwing you onto the ground, and eating you out wherever I find you. Once you come home, though, you're mine. Do us both a favor and don't invite your little friend back here, alright? I'll take care of the rest."

Wow. Seriously, wow. I don't even know what to say. I just stare at him, and Ethan stares back at me. His eyes are radiant and blue. I'm lost. In them. In his words, his look, his...

He pulls his finger out of me, past my panties, and fixes them quick. Then he helps me up off the bed and pulls my skirt back down, making it look almost normal and regular. Almost.

"Give your dear brother a kiss before you go?" he says, tapping his cheek. It's a request, but also a command.

I stand up on tiptoes and kiss his cheek. It's so oddly contrary to what we... what we've been um...

doing... almost sweet and chaste and familial, except we're anything but that at the moment.

For whatever screwed up reason, I feel closer to Ethan than I've ever felt before. For whatever screwed up reason, I really like that, too.

Mia Clark

4 - Ashley

S ORRY ABOUT BEFORE," Julia says to me.

"Huh?" I ask.

After my heart to heart with Ethan, Julia and I left the house to get lunch and go shopping. Nothing too crazy, just a nice little outlet mall nearby. I like the dresses at this one store, and... they have a nice selection of lingerie, too. Which... I might go look at in a second... maybe...

Just for me, you know? A girl has to treat herself sometimes. I don't have any plans for this. It's not like I want to show it to anyone, or dress up sexy for anyone, or...

Yeah, um... I don't know what I'm doing anymore. I just...

"I didn't mean to be so um... open?" Julia says. "I don't know. I know Ethan is your brother now. That must be weird, huh?"

"Stepbrother," I tell her; and I feel like this is a good reminder for me, too. Again. "It's been a couple of years since our parents married," I add. "It's not like it's some all of a sudden thing."

"Yeah, I guess so. I never really thought about it before, though. Must be hard, huh?"

"What?" I really have no idea what she's saying.

"You know, um... with him walking around shirtless like that? Don't you stare? Er... that's weird, isn't it? Since he's like your brother and um... your parents are married now, and..."

"Yeah," I say. Be casual, Ashley. Cool and smooth. "Ew. Gross."

That's it. Ew and gross are proper words to describe staring at your brother with lust. Or having sex with him. Stepbrother. What the heck? I need to stop this. It really is getting weird. I can't just fantasize about...

Is he really going to do that? If I texted him right now and told him what store I was at, that I was about to try on some lingerie, would he seriously come here, drag me into a changing room, and...

Eat me out?

Oh my God. Wow. Um...

"I just think it'd be hard," Julia says. "I mean, I understand, you know? That it's weird. His dad and your mom. I don't know if I could help myself, though. I'm kind of interested, aren't you?"

"Huh?" Again, I'm confused. Where is she going with...?

"He's got a reputation and everything. I know he's kind of an asshole. Everyone says it, and he acts the part, so it's not like I'm saying he isn't. I'm just saying that um... if I know he's an asshole, and I don't go into it with any expectations, well... everyone says he's really good in bed, too, so..."

"Julia! Seriously? Why are we having this conversation?"

"I mean... would you mind if I...? I'm just curious!"

"Yes," I say. "I mind."

"Just once?" she asks. "I won't even tell you about it, I won't talk about it, Ashley, I swear. I just kind of... I mean, Ethan is hot! For real."

"I'm not going to give you permission to have sex with my brother," I say.

"Stepbrother," Julia adds.

"Whatever."

I'm done. This is done. I go back to poking through these cute summer dresses. They're nice. There's a few that I'm not too sure about. Strapless ones. I like those, but sometimes they can be a pain. It's not that I have huge breasts, but... they're big enough to sometimes cause issues with something like that. Ooh, but there's some cute strapless bras over there, too. I should try those on. And then...

Lingerie. I can rationalize this one to Julia, I think. I don't have to mention it's for anyone. I told her a little about what happened with Jake, so I can just say I want to get something sexy to make me feel better, to make me feel sexier even if I don't have a boyfriend right now.

Which is true. Sort of. I don't have a boyfriend, but I have someone I wouldn't mind being sexy for. Does that count? She doesn't have to know that.

"What if it's just a blowjob?" she asks. "Like, no penetration? If he fingers me is it alright? Or what if he goes down on me? Does that count?"

You know what, Julia? He's going down on *me* as soon as I get home! And, yes, I like hanging out with you, but, no, you can't have my brother. Ethan is mine. For this week. He's...

I don't say any of this, I just give her a nasty look. She sighs and shakes her head.

"It's just such a waste," she says. "I get why you can't do anything with him, but I don't know why I can't take advantage of it. We're friends, aren't we?"

I laugh. Yes, um... if only she knew...

"It's just weird," I say. "I have to live with him, too, you know? What if you fall in love with him? I know you say you won't, but a lot of girls said that in high school, right?"

"Yeah, well, we both know how he is," she says, matter-of-fact.

"Yeah," I agree.

"It doesn't matter who falls in love with Ethan Colton. He'll sleep with them for a couple of weeks, then dump them and never return their calls. Remember when we tried to figure out if there was some astrological equation to it?"

I laugh. "I can't believe we did that. It was so stupid."

"Yeah," she says, snickering. "Like, maybe it had to do with the alignment of the stars? If you go on a date with Ethan at a certain time of the month, during a certain time of the year, then you can figure out how to make him fall in love with you. Every girl would have loved to know if that was true."

"What about the werewolf theory?" I asked. "That was a good one, too."

"Yeah, didn't work, though. It was never the same time. A couple of times he ditched girls when it was a full moon, but it never happened regularly."

"Maybe we should have tried tea leaves?" I suggest.

"Shit, we never did that, did we?" Julia says. "I don't even know how to read tea leaves."

I shrug and giggle. "Me either. Could be fun to try, though?"

"You want to? We can get some tea and go back to your place?"

"Um... maybe another time. I'm still uh... I'm just not feeling up to it right now, after what happened with Jake, you know?"

Actually, I'm not feeling up to it right now because of what's going to happen with Ethan, but she really doesn't need to know that one, now does she?

"I understand," she says. "Ooh, hey, you want to look at lingerie? That'll make you feel better. Sexy and confident! It's cute, too."

You read my mind, Julia!

"Sure," I say, trying not to sound too excited. "That could be fun."

"I'll get something, too. You know, just in case. I wish I had someone to show it off to, though. Like, um..."

"Seriously, don't even say it."

She doesn't. Not for a few seconds. Not until we're standing next to a rack of sexy, sheer negligees.

"Like Ethan."

5 - Ethan

HOLY FUCK, this pussy is gold.

When Ashley comes home I'm ready. I don't plan on fucking around with this. I feel like I need to make up for lost time, even though I never expected to be doing this in the first place. You know who she is? She's Ashley "Good Girl" Banks. Little Miss Perfect. A Goddamn Fucking Princess.

Basically what I'm saying is she shouldn't end up in bed with a guy like me. I'm not good. Yeah, I do alright sometimes. I can't say I'm the worst ever. I don't expect to join some biker gang or go to jail any time soon, so I guess I have that going for me, but I'm not the kind of guy who has relationships. I don't do feelings. There's no falling in love. Everything with me is a lot more primal and basic.

We're going to fuck. Hard. No condoms. Rule number eight. Shit, I love rule number eight.

Let me take a step back for a second and say that I only like rule number eight because it's with Ashley. I understand the importance of protection. I've never even had the urge to fuck around with that shit. The girls I'm usually with are... alright, they're nice girls, don't get me wrong, but I don't trust them.

Ashley's different. Don't take that the wrong way. I'm not going to explain any of this to you. It doesn't matter. It's not just her, but it's what I want to do to her, and what I want to show to her, too.

Sex with condoms isn't horrible or anything. It's fine. Yeah, it feels fucking amazing without them, and that's the point. Doesn't just feel nicer for me, but it's going to feel nicer for her, too. And I want her to remember that.

The next time she has some guy's cock deep inside her, I want her to know what she can look forward to. What she can expect in a good relationship. Something nice, something long term, where they're committed and they don't have to use condoms anymore, and they can seriously just fucking enjoy each other to the fullest, and...

Nevermind. I take that back. I don't want to think about this shit. Don't get me wrong, I do want her to understand what pure ecstasy is like, but after me she probably won't. No offense to all the other men in the world, but I'm Ethan Colton, and you just can't compete. That's how it is. Sorry fellas.

Anyways, this is done. I'm through. Ashley walks in the door and good fucking thing Julia isn't with her, because I've been waiting all day for this shit. I grab her, caveman-style, and drag her to the game room. Nice place, great room. It's got a pool table in the center, with darts off to the side, a TV for watching sports, a couch, card table area. Big room.

My dad and I used to play pool and watch football on the weekends. Sometimes we'd order takeout, or make nachos, and once we were done goofing off, we'd chill on the couch, just sit back. I remember falling asleep more than once, waking up with a blanket over me, my dad sleeping on the floor beneath me, giving me the couch to myself.

That was before. He got busy later, and I still watched football and screwed around, but it was just me at home, sometimes with a babysitter or whatever the fuck you want to call them, adult supervision. I don't know what happened, but things changed.

Oh well, it happens, right? That's life.

Yeah, so, Ashley and I are going in the pool room, but there's no games happening now. Not that kind, at least. I'll play some games with her, alright, but we're both going to be winners here. Lots and lots of fun.

"Ethan!" she shrieks, but I can tell she's into it. Laughing, giggling, squirming side to side. Fuck, the way she moves makes me hard. I want her to shriek and scream and squirm like that with my cock deep inside her. Say my fucking name, Princess.

"You're mine now," I say, grinning.

"What are you doing?" she says. Still shrieking.

I gently, carefully, forcefully, roughly (some combination of those, who knows?) toss her onto the pool table. She lands on her back, arms flailing, legs splayed out.

"You need to get these off of you," I say. "Now."

I grab her skirt and pull. It's still tight around her waist, but do you think I care? Nah. I keep pulling, stretching it, forcing it down her hips. She finally gets the memo, realizes what's up, and starts to undo it so I can get it off of her without ripping it. Good fucking riddance. Goodbye skirt. Hello Ashley's gorgeous fucking pussy.

This girl is a freak. Absolute freak. I know she had panties on earlier. Where'd they go? I don't know, but they aren't there now.

Glistening like pure gold, shiny and wet, I just stare at the beautiful work of art in front of me. She fidgets, stuck between being shy and wanting to show off for me. Her legs slip apart slightly, giving me a little show, then she clamps them shut again, hiding. Fuck, it's the sexiest thing I've ever seen.

I'm hard. I was hard before, but my erection has an erection right now, if you catch my drift. Maybe more than one. I keep my pants on, though. This isn't about that. Down boy, you'll get your turn later. I've got things to show this girl that just can't wait.

"You remember what I said before?" I ask her. "About what I asked you?"

She glances up at me and bites her lower lip, then nods. "Mhm."

"I need to be straight with you, Ashley. I want to bury my tongue inside your pussy and eat you out until you're cumming so hard that you scream my name and you're so loud that the neighbors call the cops."

"Ethan," she says, coy, confused, and cute; some of my favorite C words right there. "The nearest neighbors are a mile away. I don't think--"

"Exactly," I say. "You're not thinking. Think a little harder, Princess. Which is it? You don't think they'll hear you, or you don't think I can do a good enough job to make you scream loud enough so that they'll hear you. Answer wisely."

Her eyes widen. Shit, she's beautiful. Absolutely gorgeous. I love her eyes. I love the way her lip curls a little, the way it is now, and then she opens her mouth slightly, shocked. I want to kiss her. Yeah, you know what?

I have a week. My week. Our week. I'll do what I want.

I prowl onto the table above her, pressing hard against her. My hips grind against her, my pants-covered cock pressing against her bare pussy. Then my lips. On hers. Hard.

I kiss her. This is love. Temporary, yeah. I guess you could call it lust, and that's a fine word, but I think temporary love is nicer. Poetic, you know? Ephemeral and fleeting, like a midsummer night's dream. Shakespeare was quite the cunning linguist, don't you think? I'm gonna be something like that with Ashley, and I want her to know it.

My tongue tastes hers, her mouth, her lips. I love the taste of her. She's sweet and innocent, like ripe peaches. I back off to see what she does, but she doesn't let me go. Her hands wrap around my neck, pulling me back to her. Yeah, that's it. Good girl...

She closes her eyes and savors everything. I do the same, but different. I move, my body pressing and grinding against hers. I want to see how she'll react. I want to see what she does. I thrust my hips forward, digging my cock against her pussy, rubbing up towards her clit, then further up along her pubis. She follows my every move, lifting her hips, trying to match my moves with ones of her own.

Fucking beautiful. She's really good at this for someone who doesn't have a lot of experience. It's a simple sort of passion, though. Personally, I think that's the best kind. It's not fake or intentionally harsh, it's just natural and perfect. I move, she moves, and that's that. We don't have to get too crazy here, we just need to be on the same wavelength.

Get on my level, Princess. I'll take you to a place you've never been before, one you can't even imagine...

I stretch my hand down and tease it up her side. She's still got her tanktop on, but I like that. Shirts are great. They're fun to lift, just so, pulling them up, keeping part of her covered while I reveal the rest. Her bare, silken skin tightens at my touch as she shifts and moves, fighting between squirming away and moving in close. More, I pull it up, then I slip my hand underneath, moving towards her breast.

She took her panties off sometime after she left, but she's still got her bra on. Good. I don't want anyone else seeing these. I don't care if she has a shirt on. They're mine. No one should even ever get a glimpse of her pert, hard nipples, cloth-covered or not. I move in for the kill, cupping her breast in my palm, squeezing her nipple between my fingers. To test her, for good measure, I squeeze harder than I should.

She opens her mouth to say something, or to let out a pained gasp, and then she does the most sexy as fuck thing I can think of.

Little Miss Perfect bites me. My lip. Hard, but not hard enough to break the skin. Just enough to let me know what's going on, what she's doing. I don't even know if she does it on purpose or not. I squeeze her nipple harder, intoxicated by this sudden turn of events, and she moves her hands from behind my neck to my back, digging her fingernails into my shirt and my skin, clawing at me.

Fuck, yes, this is amazing.

I almost do it. I almost let her go, rip my pants off, and bury my erection inside of her without any more thought to it than that. I fucking need her pussy like I need my own heart to keep beating. I'm going to die without it. I can't keep living. I swear to God it's impossible.

Sometimes it's fun to hold your breath, though. You ever try that? Just go in the pool, go underwater, see how long you can hold your breath? It's a test, a game, and it's somewhat of a calculated risk. It's fun to see how much you can take before you break and come up to the surface, though.

This is like that. I want to see how much I can take before I give in. I want to see how much she can take before she begs me to fuck her.

I sneak away from our kiss, even though she's doing everything she can to keep me there. Her lips pout and beg, kissing at air, trying to bring me back to her. Not today, Princess. Or, not yet, at least.

"We're going to play a game," I tell her.

"Ethan," she says, whimpering, batting her eyelashes at me. Yeah, fuck, she just batted her eyelashes at me. I'm going to die. "I don't want to play pool. I want you to make love to me."

Make love? Yeah, I don't know, maybe that's what we'll do. Sometime. Not now. I can be gentle when I want, when the mood suits the situation. Right now I want to be rough, though. Right now I want to fucking manhandle this girl, devour her pussy, and make her cum harder than any girl has a right to cum.

"Not that kind of game, Princess," I say, smiling. I kiss her quick, but pull back fast enough that she can't catch me and keep me there. "I'll kiss you again, don't worry. A little lower. You stay here, don't even worry about it, alright?"

"Lower?" she says, confused. Then it dawns on her and her eyes open wide.

God, I could drown in her eyes. They're the color of a dark, golden brown sunset just after dusk when the sky turns black, complete with a faint twinkle of starlight shining through.

I catch myself staring at her too long. I don't know what happened there.

"One of us is going to crack," I tell her. "I'll be down here--" As if she didn't already realize, I reach down and pat lightly against her pussy, letting her know exactly where I'll be. "And I'll be doing my best to make sure you're the one who breaks. You just tell me when, but don't go half-assed with this. I won't come up until you're begging and pleading with me to fuck you."

"What about you?" she asks, almost innocent, sweet as fuck. "What if you break first?"

"You think I'm going to be the one who breaks? You don't have a high opinion of me, do you, Princess?"

She smiles, shy, and turns away. "No, I... I was just wondering, that's all."

"It's fine," I say, kissing her cheek. "You want to know a secret?"

She nods, fast. "What is it?"

"You just might be the girl who gets me to break first."

Why? Why did I say that? I don't know. I can't fucking tell you. Shit, how fucking cheesy was that? I need to redeem myself.

Unfortunately, it's true. I'm fine. I can usually contain myself. I can do what I need to do, get the job done, and then take my own pleasure later. For some reason, Ashley does things to me, though. I can't stop thinking about her. Everything. All of her. I can't stop thinking about how fucking amazing it felt when my cock was deep inside of her, when she was cumming, pulling me in, her wet arousal coating my shaft. I can't stop remembering how fucking good she felt, how amazing it was to slam into her, balls deep, and fill her with my seed.

It's the condoms, I bet. Or lack thereof. That's what has me strung up and on edge. Makes sense, right?

Yeah, that's what I'm going with. That's what it's got to be.

I'm not sure. I don't think it is. Don't fuck with me on this, though. I don't have time for your shit.

She's beaming. Bright as fuck, smiling like the sun, gazing at me with lust and adoration. There's another word for that, but I don't know what it is. Figure it out yourself. I'm busy here.

"If I break, it's because I can't handle it anymore," I tell her. "It's because you're screaming and writhing and moaning on this table and it'll be the most erotic and sexual thing I've ever seen, and I just can't handle it anymore. At which point I'll come up, sheath my cock deep inside your pussy, and find out just what the fuss is all about, baby girl."

"Princess," she says.

"You want me to call you Princess?" I ask. "I thought you hated it?"

"I thought..." She hesitates. What's going through that beautiful little mind of hers? I want to know. "I always thought you were making fun of me. It sounds like you are."

I smirk. "Nah, I'd never make fun of you, Princess."

That does it. Good. We're back on track now.

She rolls her eyes at me, but she smiles, too. "Now I know you're lying. You've made fun of me ever since we met in the second grade. I don't know if you know this, but everyone says you're not a very nice person, Ethan Colton."

"Oh yeah? What do you say?" I ask.

"Do you want to know something?" she asks.

"Yeah," I say. "I do. Tell me."

"I used to think... well, my mom told me that whole thing where little boys tease and make fun of little girls they like. She said it was their way of getting the girl's attention."

"You thought I was trying to get your attention?" I ask, grinning. This is genuinely amusing to me. Huh.

"Maybe," she says. "A little. But... that was then. I know you better now."

"You do, do you?" I ask.

"Ethan, I like this," she says. "I do. I *really* like this. It's a little strange, and maybe it's wrong, but I... I like this. You know, with you? Um..."

"But you're scared," I say. I know what she's thinking. I know what she wants to say. "Because of what I do."

"Yes," she says.

"I don't want to be a jerk," I tell her. "You know that, right? It's not like I want to hurt anyone. This is just who I am. I'm a selfish prick."

She laughs a little, but looks away. Why am I saying this shit to her?

"Ashley, I do like you," I say. I take her chin in my hand and tilt her head back so I can kiss her. "Listen, I don't want to hurt you. That's why we're doing it like this, alright? That's why we've got these rules. It's so you know beforehand, so I won't hurt you."

"Will we still be friends after?" she asks me.

Wh... uh. What? Where the fuck did that come from?

The look on my face must give me away, because she adds, "Friends with benefits, right? But after um... the benefits are gone, can we... I know we aren't really friends. I mean, I don't know if you ever thought of me as one, and I never really thought of you as one, and we've never really hung out except for at home with Mom and Dad, so..."

"You want to be friends?" I ask her. "After," I add, "because, seriously, I want to fuck the shit out of you right now."

"Real romantic, Ethan!" she says, laughing and slapping at my shoulder.

There's something going on. It hurts, and I don't know what it is. It's just everything. I can't stop staring at her, can't stop thinking about the way she feels beneath me, can't stop thinking about how hard she makes me, can't stop thinking about...

I don't have these conversations with girls. Ever. They try to have them with me, but I don't have them with them. I grunt. I push it off. Later. Or I leave. I tell them I have shit to do. Bye. I'll text you sometime.

I don't know why I'm having this conversation with Ashley. Little Miss Perfect. Goodie two shows. It's just...

"Yeah, we can be friends," I say.

"Good," she says. "Now when does this game start?"

"Oh, you want to start, do you? Not sure why you're in a rush to lose, Princess."

"I'm not going to lose!" she says, shaking her head, fast.

"You don't think so?"

"Nuh uh."

"Let's just fucking see about that..."

6 - Ashley

'M EXCITED. I'm beyond excited. It's like my birthday and Christmas on the same day, but even more than that, too. This has never happened to me before. I've never felt like this before.

It's not just because of... because of what Ethan is about to do to me. Yes, I'm *very* excited about that, but it's more than that, too. I know I don't have a lot of sexual experience, and I know Ethan has um... quite a bit more, but the little that I do have has never involved anything like this.

I didn't know how to ask, first off. Is that something you can do? Just ask if... if... I blush at the mere thought of it, because I don't even know how someone could do that.

I think the problem is that I don't exactly understand sex. It's not that I don't like it, because I think it's fine. Or, I thought this before, but with Ethan it's...

It's more. So much more.

This isn't about the oral sex, though I'm definitely excited about that. It's about the attention. This is about me, plain and simple, and Ethan has made it about me. He is about to focus solely on my pleasure and my pleasure alone, and that's something I've never really had before. No one's ever done that for me, and the idea of it is overwhelming to say the least. It's exhilarating and amazing and exciting and...

I just don't understand, though. Why? Maybe I should lay back and enjoy this, and I am definitely going to enjoy it, but I can't help but ask myself why he's doing this, too?

Why haven't any of the other boys I've been with seemed interested in doing it? In... in going down on me, in eating me out, in... as Ethan so politely put it, devouring my pussy. My God, even the way he said it is exciting.

I thought I was a good girl, but then why do I love hearing all of the naughty things he says he wants to do to me? Why do I like him asking me what I want him to do to me, too? I'm not sure any of this is good.

No, Ashley, of course it's not good. I have to remind myself of what we're doing. This is just for a week. I've agreed to be friends with benefits with my stepbrother for a week.

It's just a week. What's the worst that can happen. Right? Um...

I'm still not sure why, though. Why is Ethan so patient with me? Why is he so focused on making me feel good? I didn't expect that. I thought he was a jerk, an asshole, a bonafide prick, and yet here he is, making sure I feel good, giving me experiences that I've never had before, ones that I've wanted, but never knew how to ask for. And the worst part is he makes it seem so easy.

I like Ethan. A lot. I've realized this over the past couple of days we've been back home, and it's shocking, but I don't know how else to feel, either. Yes, it's sex. It's supposed to be just sex. Except he said we could be friends after, and that's different from sex, isn't it? Yes, of course it is. Also, this isn't *just* sex, it's friends with benefits. It's...

Why doesn't he have a girlfriend? Why doesn't he stay with anyone for longer than a couple of weeks? Why does he always dump them after, if you could even call what they were doing dating, which I'm pretty sure is not what he would call it.

I think he should. I think he would make some girl very happy, and even if he's trouble, even if he has a mouth fit for a sailor, even if he's crude and rough and crass, he's... he's not so bad. He's attentive, he's interested. He's kind, I think, except then why would a kind person do what he does to girls? Am I different?

No. I know this, too. This is what every girl probably tells themselves. Am I the different one? Can I change Ethan Colton? Am I the one?

Of course not. I... I know this, but...

Wait. Of course *I'm* not the one. I meant other girls. I don't know what I'm doing. What I'm thinking, what I'm...

Oh my God did he really just do that? Yessssss...

My mind is at a disconnect, trapped between trying to figure Ethan out and dealing with the beautiful sensation of his lips on my body. When he stops kissing me, when we stop talking and he begins our *game*, he shifts down the pool table. Lifting my shirt, he kisses from just beneath my breasts, slow and light, a trail of lingering kisses down my stomach. He slows even more, taking a break near my belly button, trailing light kisses all across my stomach.

Just when I think I've figured some of Ethan out, just when I'm asking myself why he doesn't have a girlfriend, he goes lower again. Down, to my pubis, kissing me there. His lips trail across the hood of my clit, slow and sweet. He peeks out his tongue and licks at my sensitive little pearl. My mind snaps away from all thoughts of why Ethan is the way he is, and instead turns to what Ethan is doing at this very moment.

It's easier to understand *that*. I definitely like it. This is like before when he shaved me bare, but very different, too. His tongue traces across my bare pussy, lapping at my smooth skin. He takes tentative, light licks at my clit. I shiver and shake at each gentle lap. It's... this is very different than anything I've ever experienced before.

I was excited to experience it, and now I'm excited to be experiencing it.

"Ohhhh," I say, letting out a lusty moan.

Ethan pauses for a second. "You like that, Princess?"

I bite my bottom lip and nod. "Mhm."

"There's more where that came from, don't worry."

I'm not. I'm not worrying. I... I know this is odd, but I feel like I never have to worry about him. About what he's doing. About what he's thinking.

Not for a week, at least. After that?

I don't want to think about it. This is now and then is then. I want to live in the moment, to experience everything I can before the inevitable.

I relax and release my inhibitions and give in to Ethan's sinful desires. They're my sinful desires now, too.

He grabs my thighs tight in his arms. He has large hands, I realize. I must have known this before, but I never really realized it until now. His fingers wrap around most of my thigh, holding me tight, and he pulls my legs up and apart, giving himself better access to...

Oh my God. Wow.

Quick and fleeting, Ethan licks from the very bottom of my sex, all the way up my slit, to the top of my clit. My entire body shudders at the sexual sensation pressing through me.

"Fuck," Ethan says. "You taste so fucking sweet, Princess."

He goes back down, swirling his tongue around my labia, tasting every crease and fold, each intimate curve. Then in, tasting me, licking inside of me. His tongue is rough, but soft, and the feel of it inside me is unlike anything I've ever felt before.

He moves back up again, carefully circling my clit, but not actually touching it. I can see what he means by this being a game, too. It's building, my anticipation is, and I find myself counting each second as I await the inevitable. As I wait for him to...

There! Yessss...

His tongue peeks out, licking against my clit, pressing at the curves of my clitoral hood, then up and around. Then on my clit directly. Pressing hard, his tongue flattening. This... this is a lot. I can feel everything, his wetness, my wetness, his tongue shifting and moving, rippling and rocking against my clit.

I love it. I love this. I love...

He stops, teasing lower again. He tastes my sweet arousal. This is what he meant, isn't it? Devouring my pussy? The description fits perfectly. It's like Ethan can't get enough of me, like he wants to taste all of me, like he's feeding off my arousal, gaining energy and sustenance from my sexual need. I'm not surprised. I wouldn't be surprised if this is exactly what he's doing. I think it is. I think this is how it must always be with him.

He's attentive and sweet and caring and considerate and focused and oh my God he's suck-ing my clit into his mouth.

I did not expect this. I don't even know what this is. I didn't know this was something people did, but here Ethan is, doing it. He licks at my clit, then sucks it between his lips. His teeth tap lightly around the outer edges, nibbling my sensitive little pearl. It's a strange, sharp sensation, almost too much, almost more pleasure than I can bear. There's a border, apparently, where too much pleasure becomes almost painful, and I think we're about to cross it, but I don't think Ethan will. I think he knows exactly what he's doing, and a few seconds later he proves this to me.

The tip of his tongue flicks against my clit in rapid succession while he holds me in his mouth, then he lets me loose but keeps flicking. This is too much. I don't know what's going on. My entire body is trembling. My legs start to shake, but Ethan is still holding my thighs. That doesn't keep my feet from spasming and kicking. I reach beneath me to grab something, but my fingers only touch against the soft felt of the top of the pool table. I try to dig my nails in anyways, but it doesn't work.

"You can't give up yet," Ethan says with a smirk. "I'm just getting started. At least let me give you an orgasm first."

I shake my head at him. "I'm not," I say. "You're going to be the one to give up."

"Challenges are boring, Princess. Especially coming from someone who's all talk. Actions speak a whole lot fucking louder than words."

I know why he would think this. I do. He thinks he can turn me into a melting puddle of sexual need and desire, that he'll have me begging for him soon enough, and maybe he will, but I'm going to try. Maybe I'll give in to him easily, but I'm going to do my best to be his equal, to be a challenge, to be...

I don't know if I can do this! Oh my God what is he doing?

His tongue circles my clit again, and I've come to expect what's coming next. I like it. It's exciting and fun and it feels amazing. But apparently there's more, too. Inside me, two fingers, he pushes them past my arousal-slick folds, pressing them deep into me. It's so sudden and unexpected. My body tenses immediately, my pussy clenching against this new intrusion. I can feel Ethan's grin pressing against my pubis as he sucks my clit between his lips again.

Not until he gives me an orgasm? Well, that didn't exactly take long, now did it?

Yesss....

I shudder and spasm on the table, my body convulsing. Inside me, Ethan teases his fingers up, slow and gentle, but persistent and greedy. In his mouth, my clit throbs, and he sends pounding waves of pleasure through my body with each tap of the tip of his tongue against my pleasure pearl. I can feel the beating of my heart and soul inside his mouth.

He's like some demon, an incubus of the night, coming for me, the nubile young maiden. He has me in his clutches, more than able to trap and devour my essence, but he's teasing and toying with me instead.

I can't really say I don't like it. I love this. My body loves this. I am the sole focus of Ethan's sexual energy and attention, and it's the nicest and best and most amazing thing anyone's ever done for me. I feel empowered and full and...

The pool balls in each of the pockets on the outer edge of the pool table rattle and shake against each other. That's from me, isn't it? My body, my shaking, my trembling orgasm as Ethan thrusts his fingers inside of me and sucks on my clit. *Yes, yes it is.*

I peak, higher, higher still. This is insane to me. It's too much. So much pleasure. An excitement overload. I want to hold something. To grab something. My hands slam against the pool table, trying to dig in again, but I can't, and then I realize there's something I can definitely grab right now.

Quick, before I change my mind, because I really don't think good girls do anything like this, I grab the back of Ethan's head. It's soft and nice, but I can hold him, too. I can grip and pull and... I do.

More. I pull him onto me, pull his face against me. He gives in to me willingly, following me, pleasuring me.

I like that. I... I don't want to think about this right now, but if I did something like that to Jake, he would yell at me. He'd pull my hands away and look at me with anger and annoyance, and he'd yell at me and ask me what do I think I'm doing.

Ethan would never do that. Not like that, never like that. Ethan knows. He understands. Ethan is the epitome of "in the moment" and when someone acts in the moment with another person who is also acting in the moment, it's a thing of beauty. It's natural and primal, but amazing and artistic, too. This is us. This is our sexual creativity, our instinctive artistry, and it makes us beautiful and special.

We're beautiful and special when we're together.

My orgasm calms, almost fading, but Ethan refuses to give up. For a little while, at least. I think he's going to keep going, and I think I'm about to give in to him and ask him to stop, to come up here, to take me, but...

"Fuck it," he says. He stops, then leaps onto the table, crawling on hands and knees above me. He grabs my thighs again and pulls them apart, taking a firm spot between my legs.

When did he...?

Fast. He's very fast. Sometime after he said "Fuck it," between then and climbing atop the pool table, climbing between my legs, Ethan removed his pants. He lets go of my legs and grabs the bottom of his shirt, lifting it up and over his head. He flings it to the ground, leaving himself naked in front of me. His cock bobs and bounces, tapping against my pubis and the bottom of my stomach.

Ethan is very erect. Very very erect. Hard. I want him inside me so badly, but...

He manages to hold off. I can see it in his eyes. There's need and lust there, a fierce glimmer of sexuality. He leans over me, hands grabbing at my tanktop. His cock lodges between us, trapped between my stomach and his, throbbing and pulsing like some living beast. That's what Ethan is, I think. A beast. Some sort of sex-crazed animal.

My mind floats to the story of Beauty and the Beast. I don't know if it fits. It probably doesn't. I'm not sure what I'm doing or why I'm thinking this. I don't have time to think about it for long.

Ethan pulls me up and rips off my shirt, tossing it away. He stares down at me, hard, eyes drinking in all of me. Pulling himself back up, admiring my body, he grabs both of my breasts, one in each hand, and squeezes them roughly.

"Give in, Princess," he says. "Do it. I want you to grab my cock and guide me inside of you. Don't make this any more difficult than it has to be."

This is it. Our game. He wants me to give in, even though I think he wants to give in, too. Why? To keep control, I think. And if I'm being honest, I want nothing more than to do exactly what he says, but...

No, I don't want to lose this game. I think I can win it. Maybe. I'm not sure yet.

I shake my head and bite my lip. No.

He glares at me, huffing, nose flaring. "Little Miss Fucking Perfect thinks she can beat me at my own game? What a fucking joke. I can tell you want this, Princess. You're wetter than a fucking under-water waterfall."

It's hot. And funny. I don't mean to, but I laugh. "Underwater waterfall?" I ask, giggling.

He softens, smirking at me. "This isn't funny," he says. "I want to fuck you, but you won't give in. Come on, just reach down and grab my cock. It's easy. I won't think any less of you, Princess."

I shake my head again, no. "I'm a good girl, Ethan."

He roars with laughter. "Oh yeah? I'm not so sure about that. I don't think a good girl would end up naked on a pool table while letting her step-brother devour the shit out of her perfect little pussy, do you?"

"No," I say, agreeing. "I think you're forgetting something, though. One of the virtues of a good girl is that we're patient. It's like how they say nice guys finish last? Well, I think we both know who the nice one is here."

"Holy fuck," Ethan says, grinning. "Holy fucking fuck. Wow. I can't even believe this."

I smile. "I'll give in if you kiss me," I say.

"I'll kiss you when you give in," he counters.

We are, it seems, at an impasse.

Or not.

Ethan has an idea, apparently. It turns out to be a very good idea. He's smart when he wants to be.

He lets go of one of my breasts and grabs my hand. I don't fight at first, because I'm not sure what he's doing, but when he wraps my fingers around his cock, I understand. I try to pull away, try to fight against him, but he wraps his fingers around mine, keeping me holding onto his erection.

"Ethan!" I shout at him, but I can't help but laugh, too.

"Yeah?" he says. "What's up, Princess?"

"This isn't fair. You're forcing me."

"Life's not fair, Princess," he says. "Get over it."

I laugh and squirm and try to free myself from him, but he's too strong and I'm trapped beneath him. He makes me guide his cock towards my sex. I can feel him, feel the head of his erection poking and prodding and...

He's in. As soon as he is, he lets me go. Sort of. He grabs my wrist and pins it above my head, then he slams hard into me and crashes down atop me. His lips meet mine just as his cock thrusts all the way inside of me. Oh my God, so good, so...

So much. So full. And his lips are so rough, but so passionate. I kiss him and my fingers clench and grab at air, my hand trapped in his wrist, begging to be free so I can...

My other hand. It's free, isn't it? Yes. I grab him, his back, rake my nails into his taut muscles and soft skin. It's gentle and rough, just like him, just like Ethan.

Ethan Colton, my stepbrother, who is currently pounding hard into me, ramming his thick cock inside my tight pussy. If I thought the pool balls tucked away in their pockets were rattling before from my trembling orgasm, well...

The cacophony of sound from the pool table is deafening, but I can barely even hear it over the sound of flesh against flesh, Ethan's hard cock pounding into my bare pussy.

It *is* nice, I realize. Just like he said. Both of us, Shaved and shaved, slick and smooth, nothing to stop us, nothing to get in the way. It's just him and I, our bodies perfect together, our mutual lust combined into one powerful, awe-inspiring, orgasmic existence.

I fade. I lose. This game is over. I think we're both winners, though.

Ethan roars out his triumph, grunting and thrusting and pounding. He pushes hard all the way inside of me and I can feel his cock twitching and pulsing, ready to fill me to the brim. I feel myself, too, just on the edge, just one little push. As soon as he cums, he sends me over the precipice of pleasure, my climax complete.

I clutch and squeeze and grab at him. Inside, my inner walls grip his cock tight, begging him for more. Outside, my lips frantically kiss at his, needing and wanting everything, all of him. He still keeps my one hand pinned above my head, but with my other I trace red, ragged lines in his back with my nails, over and over, digging into his skin.

Ethan pulls out slightly, then pounds hard back in. He holds himself there, cock twitching, still cumming, then out, a little, inch by inch, and he slams back in again.

"Fuck. You. Are. So. Fucking. Fuck," he says. I have no idea what this means but I love it and I laugh and smile and kiss him and revel in our mutual orgasms together.

"Mine," he growls in between kissing me. I nip at his lower lip, which makes him grin. "You're mine, Princess. Your pussy is fucking god-like. I don't even want to pull out ever. I want to fall asleep inside you, like a goddamn fucking pillow for my cock."

I suck his lip into my mouth even more and bite down a little harder, smiling at him.

"You have fun?" he asks, his words coming out funny with his lip in my mouth. "I took your oral virginity. How was that?"

I let go of his lip and smile and kiss him. "Good," I say. "No, it was great. Ethan, it was amazing. Is that how it always is?"

"Nah," he says, cocksure and confident. "I'm just really fucking good."

"You are," I say. "I liked it a lot."

"Oh yeah? Don't worry, there's more where that came from. A lot more."

"Oh?" I ask, coy. "Like what?"

"Like what? Holy fuck, you're insatiable, aren't you? I'm going to turn you into some kind of sex freak or something. Maybe we should stop. I don't want to be responsible for something like that."

He says this, but he grins, too. I pout and shake my head.

"No," I say. "We can't stop. I don't want to."

"No?"

"No!"

"Well, you're in luck. I'm making another rule," he says, but then he pauses.

I give him a funny look, but he doesn't say anything for a few more seconds.

"Ashley, what the fuck rule are we on now? I can't keep up with this. We need to write this shit down or something."

I laugh and lean up to kiss him. "Eleven," I tell him. "The last one was ten."

"Got it. Good. Rule number eleven, then. Here it is. You ready?"

I nod. I'm ready. I'm more than ready. I think this will be a good rule.

"Rule number eleven is that I'm going to eat your sweet fucking pussy at least once a day. At least. Maybe twice. Three times. All fucking day. What are you doing tomorrow? You free? Let's just stay in bed all day and fuck. What do you think?"

"All day?" I ask, eyes wide. Is that even possible?

"You don't think I can do it?" he asks.

I shake my head, no. I don't want to talk right now. I just want to listen to Ethan talk. I like everything he says. He's fun.

"Listen, let's just be straight with each other here," he says. "Since this morning I've had a constant hard-on, and it's because of you. Even after we had sex, I wanted to have sex again. And right now, I'm pretty sure if you give me a couple of minutes I'll be good to go again for an hour, so... yeah, all fucking day. You're so fucking... Ashley, seriously, fuck, you're perfect, I don't even..."

He stops. I loved every word he said, loved hearing it straight from him, because it's how I feel, too, but...

I think we're going too far. Maybe. I don't understand this. I don't know what we're doing anymore. I'm not sure what we've started, and I know we're supposed to finish it... in a week... but I don't know how.

This is why he leaves every girl, isn't it?

I don't want to think about that right now. I know it's impossible, especially for us, and that's why we have these rules. That's why we've come to this agreement. It's fine. I understand it.

Logically I do. Emotionally, I don't. I'm just going to have to get over that one.

I sneak up and kiss him quick. "I'm hungry," I say.

"Oh yeah?" he asks. "Hungry for what? My cock?"

"Mhm," I murmur. "But maybe also french fries?" I add.

"Fuck, that sounds good," he says. "You ever go to that place, uh... what the fuck is it called? You probably did. Everyone did after high school. Was a great place to hang out and get something to eat, go on dates or whatever, play arcade games with friends. I wonder if everything's still the same. It wasn't that long ago, huh?"

"Albertson's," I say. "I went a couple of times with some friends, but I usually came home right after school."

"Yeah," he says. "I get it. Homework. Maybe I should have done that a little more often, too."

I laugh. "Are you regretting not doing homework? Really?"

"Nah," he says. "Homework sucked. Maybe if I had a cute study partner to help me out it would have been better."

"You could have asked me," I say. "I would have helped you."

"Oh yeah?"

"Mhm."

"I would've corrupted you," he says, grinning. "It never would have worked out."

Maybe, I think, but I don't say this, I just smile at him. Maybe you would have, Ethan, and maybe I would have enjoyed it...

A NOTE FROM MIA

THE SECOND BOOK! YAY.

I had a lot of fun with this one. I love the cute and playful parts between Ashley and Ethan, haha. They're interesting, and I think the conflict between their two personalities is intense and exciting! And maybe a little arousing, too... very heated.

If I had to pick, I would say that the part I liked writing about the most was the forbidden lovers themes. I also wanted to show some change going on, too. Relationships are exciting when they're new, but how can you build up a relationship when you know it's going to end?

There's so much going on behind the scenes with these two that it gets a little crazy. Years of build up and maybe some sexual tension has brought us to this point, and now we're seeing it boil over and create some erotic chaos.

Also, it's just fun! I think Ashley and Ethan can both teach each other a lot of stuff.

Just for a week, though, right? Hmmm...

Should they stay together longer? I don't know. They might drive each other crazy. They might drive each other crazy if they don't stay together also, though. This is tough decision.

Well, what do you think? Can they be friends after this? I'm not too sure about that one.

If you liked this story, I hope you'll rate it and review it, too! Let me know what you thought about the forbidden lovers part. How about Ethan's bad boy ways? He's got some interesting ideas, even if he tends to use them for sexual purposes. How about Ashley? Should she have been so rough on Julia? Do you think she's going to end up telling her friend? Eek.

I hope you're liking this series so far, though. There's more to come, don't worry!

Thanks for reading, and I'll see you soon! (next book!)

~MIA

.

ABOUT THE AUTHOR

Mia likes to have fun in all aspects of her life. Whether she's out enjoying the beautiful weather or spending time at home reading a book, a smile is never far from her face. She's prone to randomly laughing at nothing in particular except for whatever idea amuses her at any given moment.

Sometimes you just need to enjoy life, right?

She loves to read, dance, and explore outdoors. Chamomile tea and bubble baths are two of her favorite things. Flowers are especially nice, and she could get lost in a garden if it's big enough and no one's around to remind her that there are other things to do.

She lives in New Hampshire, where the weather is beautiful and the autumn colors are amazing.

Made in the USA
Lexington, KY
08 March 2017